DISCOVER 🐾 DOGS WITH
THE AMERICAN CANINE ASSOCIATION

── I LIKE ──
GOLDEN RETRIEVERS!

Linda Bozzo

It is the Mission of the American Canine Association (ACA) to provide registered dog owners with the educational support needed for raising, training, showing, and breeding the healthiest pets expected by responsible pet owners throughout the world. Through our activities and services, we encourage and support the dog world in order to promote best-known husbandry standards as well as to ensure that the voice and needs of our customers are quickly and properly addressed.

Our continued support, commitment, and direction are guided by our customers, including veterinary, legal, and legislative advisors. ACA aims to provide the most efficient, cooperative, and courteous service to our customers and strives to set the standard for education and problem solving for all who depend on our services.

For more information, please visit www.acacanines.com, e-mail customerservice@acadogs.com, phone 1-800-651-8332, or write to the American Canine Association at PO Box 121107, Clermont, FL 34712.

Published in 2017 by Enslow Publishing, LLC.
101 W. 23rd Street, Suite 240, New York, NY 10011
Copyright © 2017 by Enslow Publishing, LLC.
All rights reserved.
No part of this book may be reproduced by any means without the written permission of the publisher.

Library of Congress Cataloging-in-Publication Data
Names: Bozzo, Linda.
Title: I like golden retrievers! / Linda Bozzo.
Description: New York, NY : Enslow Publishing, 2017. | Series: Discover dogs with the American Canine Association | Includes bibliographical references and index. | Audience: Ages 5 and up. | Audience: Grades K to 3.
Identifiers: LCCN 2015044488| ISBN 9780766077768 (library bound) | ISBN 9780766077898 (pbk.) | ISBN 9780766077621 (6-pack)
Subjects: LCSH: Golden retriever--Juvenile literature.
Classification: LCC SF429.G63 B697 2017 | DDC 636.752/7--dc23
LC record available at http://lccn.loc.gov/2015044488

Printed in Malaysia.

To Our Readers: We have done our best to make sure all website addresses in this book were active and appropriate when we went to press. However, the author and the publisher have no control over and assume no liability for the material available on those websites or on any websites they may link to. Any comments or suggestions can be sent by e-mail to customerservice@enslow.com.

Enslow Publishing
101 W. 23rd Street
Suite 240
New York, NY 10011
USA
enslow.com

CONTENTS

IS A GOLDEN RETRIEVER RIGHT FOR YOU?

Golden retrievers, or goldens, make great family pets. They get along with everyone. They are smart and good with children. It's no wonder they are one of the most popular dog breeds.

FAST FACT:
Golden retrievers are popular work dogs. Many golden retrievers assist the disabled.

Golden retrievers love to be loved.

Golden retrievers like to play and be outdoors.

A DOG OR A PUPPY?

Puppies have lots of energy. Golden retrievers are quick learners, but training takes time. If you do not have time to train a puppy, an older golden retriever may be better for your family.

FAST FACT:
Golden retrievers grow to be large in size, 55–75 pounds (25–34 kilograms).

LOVING YOUR GOLDEN RETRIEVER

Your golden retriever will need to be kept busy. Spend time playing with him. Show him love, and he will love you back.

Loving your golden retriever is easy. And he will always love you right back!

Walk or run with your golden retriever every day.

EXERCISE

Golden retrievers enjoy outdoor exercise. They need lots of room to run in a fenced-in area. They like long walks on a **leash**. Golden retrievers also like to swim and play games, like **fetch**.

FUN FACT:
Buddy, from the movie Air Bud, was played by a golden retriever.

FEEDING YOUR GOLDEN RETRIEVER

Golden retrievers can be fed wet or dry dog food. Ask a **veterinarian** (vet), a doctor for animals, which food is best for your dog and how much to feed her.

Give your golden retriever fresh, clean water every day.

Remember to keep your dog's food and water dishes clean. Dirty dishes can make a dog sick.

Do not feed your dog people food.
It can make her sick.

Your new dog will need:

a collar with a tag

a bed

a brush

food and water dishes

a leash

toys

GROOMING

Golden retrievers can have flat or wavy hair. They **shed**, which means their hair falls out. Goldens should be brushed regularly.

Your dog will need a bath every so often. A golden retriever's nails grow fast. They will need to be clipped often. A vet or **groomer** can show you how. Your dog's ears should be cleaned, and his teeth should be brushed by an adult.

WHAT YOU SHOULD KNOW

Golden retrievers are friendly with people and other pets. They are too friendly to make very good guard dogs.

Goldens love to carry things, like balls or sticks, in their mouths.

You will need to take your dog to the vet for a checkup. He will need shots, called vaccinations, and yearly checkups to keep him healthy. If you think your dog may be sick, call your vet.

A GOOD FRIEND

Golden retrievers live up to 10 to 14 years. During that time, love and care for him. If you own a golden, you will always have a friend to play with.

NOTE TO PARENTS

It is important to consider having your dog spayed or neutered when the dog is young. Spaying and neutering are operations that prevent unwanted puppies and can help improve the overall health of your dog.

It is also a good idea to microchip your dog, in case he or she gets lost. A vet will implant a painless microchip under the skin, which can then be scanned at a vet's office or animal shelter to look up your information on a national database.

Some towns require licenses for dogs, so be sure to check with your town clerk.

For more information, speak with a vet.

fetch – To go after a toy and bring it back.

groomer – A person who bathes and brushes dogs.

leash – A chain or strap that attaches to the dog's collar.

shed – When dog hair falls out so new hair can grow.

vaccinations – Shots that dogs need to stay healthy.

veterinarian (vet) – A doctor for animals.

There are many dogs, young and old, waiting to be adopted from animal shelters and rescue groups.

Read About Dogs

Books

Barnes, Nico. *Golden Retrievers*. Minneapolis, MN: Abdo Kids, 2014

Bowman, Chris. *Golden Retrievers*. Minneapolis, MN: Bellweather Media Inc., 2015.

Finne, Stephanie. *Golden Retrievers*. Minneapolis, MN: Checkerboard Library, 2015.

Websites

American Canine Association Inc., Kids Corner
acakids.com/

National Geographic for Kids, Pet Central
kids.nationalgeographic.com/explore/pet-central/

PBS Kids, Dog Games
pbskids.org/games/dog/

INDEX